Copyright © 1991 L'école des Loisirs, Paris
Translated from the French by Alexandra Bonfante-Warren
Adapted by Ann Hodgman

Published in 1991 by
Stewart, Tabori & Chang, Inc.
575 Broadway, New York, New York 10012

Library of Congress Cataloging-in-Publication Data
Rutten, Nicole.
      [Prends mon sac, Jack! English]
      A tale of two rats / illustrations by Nicole Rutten ; text by
Claude Lager.
          p.      cm.
      Translation of: Prends mon sac, Jack!
      Summary: After moving from New York to Italy, Arthur finds success
as a painter and new friends like Jack and Mario.
      ISBN 1-55670-228-0
      [1. Friendship—Fiction.   2. Rats—Fiction.   3. Artists—Fiction.
4. Italy—Fiction.]   I. Lager, Claude.   II. Title.
      PZ7.R94Tal      1991
      [E]—dc20                                                    91-14220
                                                                       CIP
                                                                        AC

Distributed in the U.S. by Workman Publishing,
708 Broadway, New York, New York 10003
Distributed in Canada by Canadian Manda Group,
P.O. Box 920 Station U, Toronto, Ontario M8Z 5P9
Distributed in all other territories by
Little, Brown and Company, International Division,
34 Beacon Street, Boston, Massachusetts 02108

Printed in Italy
10 9 8 7 6 5 4 3 2 1

# A Tale of Two Rats

Text by
CLAUDE LAGER

♦

Illustrations by
NICOLE RUTTEN

Stewart, Tabori & Chang
New York

$W$inter had come to New York. Everyone was rushing home to get warm—everyone except Arthur. "Just let me finish this painting first," he said to himself with a shiver.

"Smile!" someone suddenly called. Arthur turned around.
Standing behind him was a rat with a camera.
Arthur *didn't* smile. "Hey, I didn't say you could take my picture!" he said.
"Or a picture of my picture!"
"I'm sorry," the other rat answered. "I didn't know it was against the rules. I come from Italy.
I just wanted a shot of your picture to take home with me as a souvenir. It's so beautiful…"
Now Arthur couldn't help smiling. "You're the first person who's said anything
nice about my painting all day," he said. "My name is Arthur. What's yours?"
"Jack," the photographer replied.
"Well, Jack, aren't you freezing? I am. Let's go back to my studio and get something to eat.
I think there's a piece of cheese rind in the cupboard."

**A**rthur's studio was filled with paintings. Jack gasped when he saw them.
"I can't believe how great these are!"
"Thanks." Arthur looked a little grumpy. "I wish someone else thought so. I guess no one
wants to buy paintings of the same old stuff they see every day."
"So paint something else!" said Jack.

Arthur gave a gloomy sigh. "I paint what I see. I can't think of anything else to paint…"
Jack could see that his new friend needed cheering up. "Why don't you come back
to Italy with me?" he asked Arthur over cups of tea and stale cheese rind.
"I'll help you earn your fare. You'll have a whole new world to paint. And the food is
a lot better there than it is here."

It wasn't easy earning the money for
Arthur's ticket to Italy. "I bet this window
hasn't been washed in fifty years!" gasped
Arthur. But at last he and Jack saved up
enough. They were ready to sail!

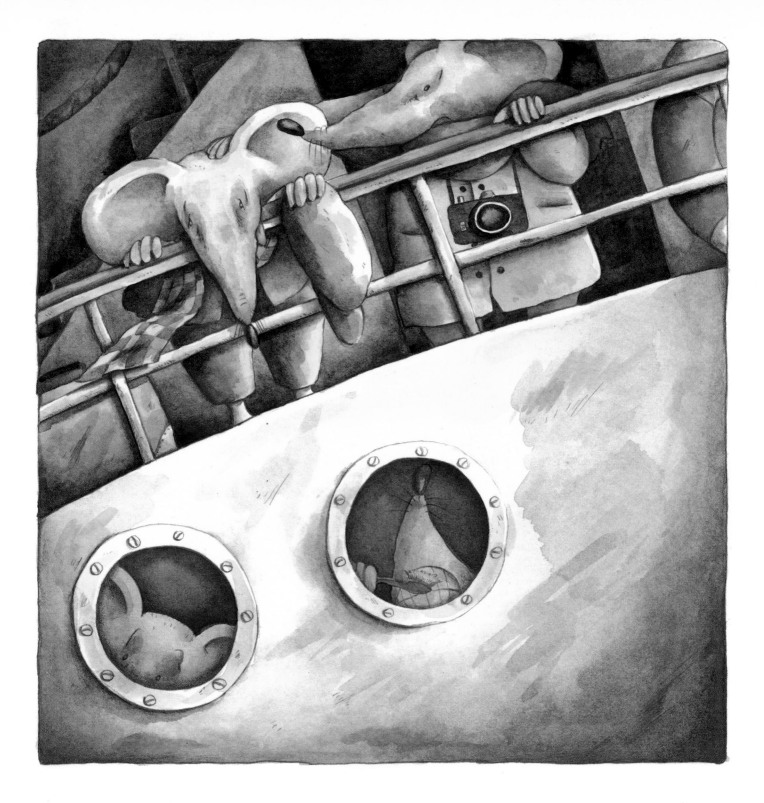

At first, the weather was terrible. "Breathe in the sea air. You'll feel better," said Jack. "I can't breathe!" moaned Arthur. "All I can do is throw up!"

Arthur felt much better when the ocean calmed. He loved sketching the sailors. And they loved posing for him. "Make sure we look busy," they always told him.

A few days later, the ship landed.
"We're home! We're home!" whooped Jack.
"ITALY, MEET MY FRIEND ARTHUR!"
"Welcome to my restaurant," bellowed
Chef Mario. "Eat! Eat! You've never
tasted food like this!" It was true.
"This is the best spaghetti I've ever had,"
said Arthur with his mouth full.
"Chef Mario, you're an artist too!" Already
he could tell he was going to love Italy.

**A**fter that, Arthur and Jack helped Chef Mario in the kitchen every night. Pizza took a lot of practice.

During the days, Arthur painted. "With this scenery, I could go on painting forever," he said happily.

One day, Chef Mario asked his friends if they'd like to come to Venice with him. "Everyone should ride in a gondola at least once. Besides, my friend Antonio runs an art gallery there," he said. "I think you two would like Venice. There's a lot going on." He was right.

"My friends, I'm leaving you in Antonio's care," said Chef Mario.

"My restaurant needs me. Come home soon!"

"Let me show you my new work," Arthur said proudly to Antonio. "Look at all the
paintings I've done in Italy! Can you sell them in your gallery?"
Antonio frowned. "They're pretty," he said.
"But why would Italians want to buy pictures of Italy?"
"Well, then, look at his paintings of New York!"
Jack pulled them out of Arthur's pack before Arthur could stop him.
"Now these are amazing," said Antonio. "Everyone will buy these."
And everyone did. Arthur was a star at last!

**B**ack home, they told Chef Mario Arthur's wonderful news.
"Let's celebrate! Pizza for everyone!" he shouted.

The next morning, Arthur woke up Jack. "Hurry! Get up! We're going back to
New York. Everyone there will love my paintings of Italy!"
"I'd be too homesick," said Jack sadly. "I'm staying."

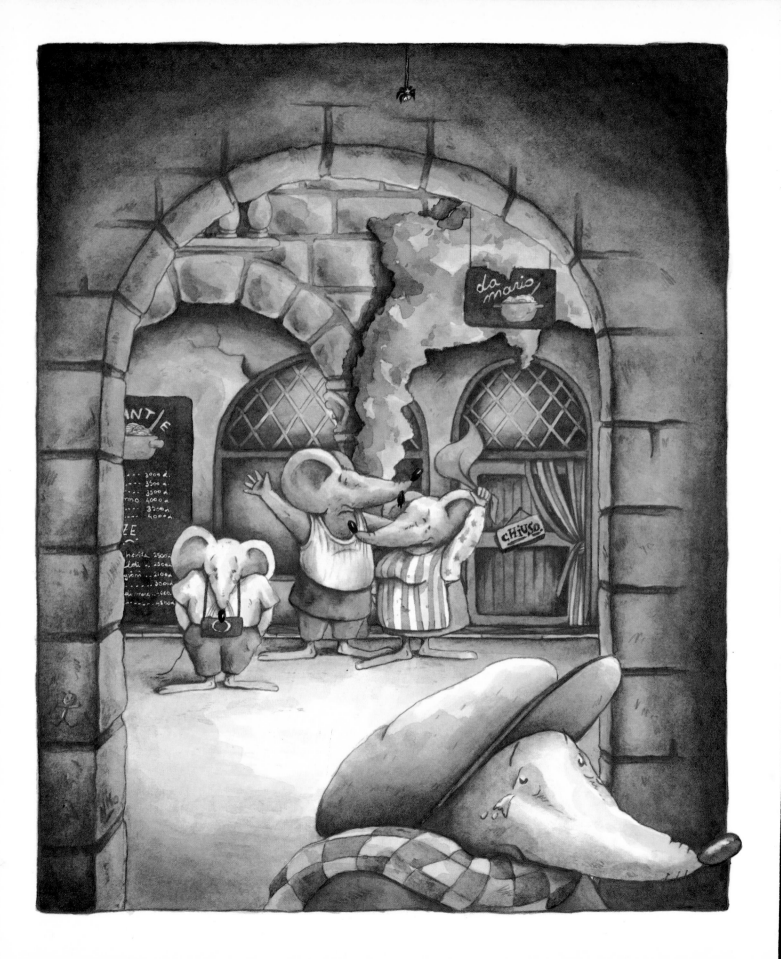

Arthur grabbed his pack. He hugged his new friends goodbye.
Then he headed for the ship…alone.
"These paintings will sell like hotcakes," he bragged to himself. "I'll be rich and
famous all over again. I love being rich and famous."
He stopped. "Of course, I'll miss Jack a lot. And Chef Mario. And pizza.
Let's not forget pizza."

**W**hen the ship sailed off to New York, it sailed without Arthur.
"Who cares about fame and fortune?" said Arthur. "I'll never find friends like these again.

**I**'m staying."